This igloo book belongs to:

....

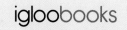

igloobooks

Published in 2017
by Igloo Books Ltd
Cottage Farm
Sywell
NN6 0BJ
www.igloobooks.com

Illustrated by Paul Nicholls
Original story by Linda Staten

Cover designed by Nicholas Gage
Interiors designed by Helen Jones
Edited by Stephanie Moss

LEO002 0217
2 4 6 8 10 9 7 5 3 1
ISBN 978-1-78670-600-3

Printed and manufactured in China

My Pet Giraffe

igloobooks

Goldie is my giraffe. He doesn't live in a zoo.

My giraffe is my best friend.

He's my **tallest** friend, too!

Goldie can't sleep in
my room, but
I don't really mind.

He sleeps in our garden shed.
It's the **tallest** we could find.

Goldie isn't like other giraffes.

He likes to relax and chill out.

He doesn't want to spend every day
stretching up high and running about.

Sometimes he gets so sleepy, that much to my surprise...

... he'll climb into my comfy hammock

and close his tired eyes.

Goldie sometimes causes trouble.

He brings strange presents to me.

He pretends that

he's a dog...

... and fetches

a branch

from a tree!

I love to eat **sticky** treats and I even let Goldie share.

People might think we look odd sometimes,

but we don't really care!

Goldie always looks out for me.

He is the most caring pet.

Giraffes always know
where to find you when
you feel upset.

I have lots of boring chores...

... but they're fun with a giraffe.

In fact, with a friend like Goldie...

... you can have a real laugh!

Goldie loves **splashing** in bubbly baths...

... though it's hard to find one to fit.

Luckily, I love having **soggy-wet** showers, so I don't mind one bit.

Reading books with Goldie is the
thing that I love best.

Giraffes love funny stories...

I love my pet giraffe. It feels so special when we're together. I just know I'm going to be best friends with Goldie **forever** and **ever**.